The Baseball Diet Book

To Peter —
the best!

SOL BOOKS UPPER MIDWEST WRITERS SERIES

The Baseball Diet Book

Pat Ryan

SOL BOOKS

Minneapolis

Published by Sol Books,
an imprint of Skywater Publishing Company,
398 Goodrich Avenue, St. Paul, MN 55102
www.solbooks.com

Library of Congress Cataloging-in-Publication Data
Ryan, Patrick, 1948–
The Baseball Diet Book / Pat Ryan.
p. cm.
ISBN 978-0-9818279-4-0 (pbk. : alk. paper)
ISBN 978-0-9818279-5-7 (ebook : alk. paper)
1. Baseball stories. I. Title.
PS3618.Y3359B37 2011
813'.6—dc22 2010034095

Acknowledgments
"The Cleveland Indian Indian", edited by John Bonnes, was published originally in *Game Day Magazine.*

"The Effey Mosquitoes" was originally published by Kristy and Wes Schuck.

Photo Credits
Shutterstock/David Lee, cover
Martha Woodward, 103

This book is dedicated to my wife
of thirty years, Martha Woodward.
All good things began with her.

Contents

Forward

If you're a baseball fan—or a non-fan with a big heart and a susceptibility to tall tales—plan on smiling through these pages. It's a reader's blessing to discover a storyteller who's as inventive, authoritive and good-hearted as Pat Ryan. If Mark Twain had been a baseball fan, and if he'd had medication to combat his bi-polar disorder, this is the kind of story he'd have written. Will Rogers, too, although I don't know if he was nuts like that. I can say nuts, because I'm nuts too. Although not as nuts as the character named Terry in Ryan's story The Schizophrenic Centerfielder. I played third.

When my granddaughter's born in October, I'll read her these stories as an intro to a kid's sweet dream of baseball; and I'll intersperse a vinyl of Blood on the Tracks, one of the great human utterances. Plus, I'll give her my old Rawlings glove. Plus, when she's twelve I'll find her an old transistor radio the size she can hold in her hand, so that when her parents make her go to bed, she can listen to games under the covers.

I know what you're thinking: "Davis, you can't write a foreword for Pat Ryan. He's your friend, for gawd's sake."

Sure I can. I don't like Pat anywhere near as much as I like good writing. I get into the world of these stories, and Pat drops out of my mind like a can o' corn the shortstop loses in the sun. This is what good stories do, of course: they pull us out of the actual world into their separate world, where a kid named Stats has a magic scorebook and controls the action of the game, say; or a Panamanian catcher named Bob entreats the Father, Son and Holy Ghost to help him hit homers, gets beaned, and in the hospital suffers a vision of the Son, who tells him that prayer is for wisdom and love, not for hitting baseballs.

Wisdom and Love. That's the battery Ryan sends to the mound. And he's got Laughter cranking up in the bullpen.

Terry Davis

Quentin Pugh

Quentin started eating Ho Ho's in 1997. He ripped open the first package when he heard that the owner of the Florida Marlins was selling off his favorite players. He was distraught. It could be argued he was just another victim of Osama Bud Selig. Selig, Commissioner of Major League Baseball since 1992, refused to reign in the payroll of the Yankees, and the game became all about big market. The Marlins owner decided to make a mockery of the World Series Trophy and show how one could buy a championship title like a trinket at a carnival.

A lifetime Red Sox fan, Quentin had moved to Miami, where he underwent his first shocking transformation: a conversion to the Marlins. In the sunshine state, he began his baseball life over with the Dream Team of the Palms. It was a joyful time for him because his new team *actually won*. The World Series, no less. And he had been there, drinking direct from the cup of the baseball gods, a toe in the filthy lucre of the Yankees Promised Land as the famed pinstripes relinquished their title. But the joy was short lived.

The high of the Series title dissolved all too quickly. In a manner that a Red Sox fan would understand, the crash came, and the Marlins owner sold off the team. The reaction to this callous fire sale was a binge. A Ho Ho's binge. It would prove to be the worst kind of craving.

Something drove him to his second package of Ho Ho's and then a third, a fourth and finally a case of 48 he special ordered from a warehouse that stocked the gas station by his house. Though he loved Ho Ho's best, he didn't limit his sugar palate. He also indulged in Dots, Gummy Bears, Snickers bars, Butterfingers, Twinkies, ice cream roll cake, Goobers, Reese's Pieces, chocolate malts, and chocolate chip cookies. But he treasured Ho Ho's the most. Ho Ho-ing his way into a sugar haze of excess, he was lost in Miami with a case of cream-filled chocolate treats. Unable to stop himself.

His sister, Ann, who wrote diet books and was something of a fitness expert, had tried to intervene, but she couldn't stop him. Years earlier she had him admitted to a treatment center in Palm Springs. He learned overeaters are prone to "triggers." His sister knew that until he learned to rewire his response to these triggers, nothing could help him. Ann was puzzled and frustrated. Nothing she knew about dieting or eating fit Quentin. She had no explanation for why he started or why he stopped.

What Ann didn't know was that Quentin stopped eating back in Boston, not because his team had won or lost, but because he read an article about Bill Buckner the famous goat who blew the World Series in 1986. Quentin began laughing after he read that Buckner sold the infamous error ball twenty times. Buckner became sort of a mentor for him. Quentin put his life in perspective, stopped eating and moved on. His current binge was a little different.

After a time, Ann realized her helping wasn't helping and could see that the current munch fest was going to be a long run. She resolved to never come back, and when she left she told him, "Go to hell and eat."

So he did.

He was a prodigious gainer. Within six months he was 300 pounds and counting. He imagined being featured on Oprah, a special leather couch that could hold him up for the show. He was heading to 400 pounds in a Ho Ho minute. Tragically, the day came when he was not able to get out of bed.

To make matters worse, Quentin was a trust fund baby, which meant he had ample means to purchase as much junk food as he pleased. The money came from his father who had been a best-selling author and sold more health books than any living person. (Much to the delight of overeaters everywhere, the elder Pugh died while jogging.) Quentin was haunted by death at an early age. He got the message: no jogging. Let Ann write and blabber about health and exercise all she wanted. Quentin didn't plan to live it.

Quentin's life was his bed. Well taken cared for by hired help, with everything delivered to him, he was like a Franz Kafka character in *Metamorphosis.* A big bug. A sumo bug.

He passed his time by watching daytime TV and playing video games. He couldn't watch nighttime television because it made him sick to his stomach. Daytime TV fit the surf and snack mode for which he was accustomed. He spent his time playing Madden and online Texas Hold 'em tournaments, until he was banned from playing poker because he was so successful. Quentin may have been fat, but he was also smart.

One afternoon between snacks he stumbled onto a baseball game online. The game was generated by a company in Osaka, Japan. He liked the format, especially the fact that the players were obscure. It was during one of his games that he learned about Mothra.

Mothra was a nickname given to the best pitcher in Japanese baseball. He was famous for his "gyro pitch." Quentin threw Mothra's virtual gyro ball in his internet games. Mothra won the league championship for him by striking out 27 batters in a game.

After winning the title, Quentin began studying the real gyro ball. Not a curve or a slider. It was an entirely new pitch. He found an informative article by a physicist from MIT. The scientist explained that if the baseball were thrown with a spiral it would create a vortex of spin that resulted in a lateral action. The ball had to be thrown less than 60 miles an hour. The slow velocity fascinated him. Most grade school pitchers throw faster. It was a classic case of "less is more." It was obvious why not many Westerners could grasp the concept.

One of Quentin's day nurses built a contraption that would allow him to lie in bed and throw the ball into a pad. The pad had a plastic tube that would roll the ball back to him, so he could practice the pitch.

It was his mission to master the "googly". He set about learning the pitch with the same sense of resolve that put him over the 400 lb. mark.

He threw pitch after pitch until blisters appeared on his fingers. He treated them with the same ointment he used on his bedsores.

One day the food courier saw him pitching. Quentin shared with him his goal to be the first American to master the gyroball. The delivery man told Quentin that he coached a group of 15 year olds and that if he could get out of his room he could arrange a batting practice.

Quentin called a rental store and arranged to have a horse trailer haul him to the field. The trailer company hired some Mexican day laborers to help load him up. He heard them chattering in Spanish, talking about *El Hombre Enorme*. The Big Man. The Big Man was going to leave the house for the first time in years.

The baseball boys were in disbelief as the trailer pulled onto their practice field. They stood with their bats on their shoulders and pondered the state of the game. First Bud Selig and now a 400 pound pitcher.

The trailer's back door slammed to the ground, and Quentin rolled onto the mound in a specially designed four wheeler. He didn't make eye contact with the boys but sat quietly on the back of the utility vehicle. He didn't want to press his luck by standing on the mound. Glove in hand; he waited for batter number one. It would not be batting practice but a pitching lesson. The pee wee players were going to see their first gyro ball.

The first batter was 5 foot 6, and Quentin hadn't planned on pitching to midgets. The kids yelled "C'mon, Shorty! Get a hit."

The Big Man wound up and threw his 50-mile-an-hour pitch to Shorty. The kid swung hard, and the ball whistled by Quentin's head and out into centerfield. He needed to grip the ball harder to get it to travel the distance. Shorty readied himself for another pitch. The ball was moving closer to sixty. Quentin's arm extended fully, and the ball blooped just before it got to the plate. Everyone saw it. The kid swung and missed. The pitch appeared to be from a different world.

Quentin went on to strike out the entire team. A new era of baseball had arrived in North America. He could tell he had mastered the gyroball, but he also realized that these kids were not professionals. He had to find a real pro.

This led him to Tokyo Joe. Tokyo Joe was a phenomenon in the Japanese league. He had recently signed with the New York Yankees. One of Quentin's old classmates from high school worked in the Yankee club house. He told Tokyo Joe about the gyro thrower and asked him if he'd be willing to do some batting practice with the Big Q. Quentin was working on some nicknames, the "Big Q" was his latest. Joe agreed to meet them at the practice field.

Joe showed up on time on his Vespa scooter. He seemed distracted to be a part of a clandestine meeting, but he had a reputation as being a generous person who would help anyone. And he could hit gyros.

After a few pleasantries, Joe was ready. The gate was unlatched and the drawbridge door slammed to the ground. The Big Q rolled out ready for work. He looked in to see where the catcher's glove was positioned. It took about five seconds for him to get all of the fat moving, but eventually the ball popped out, and it went sludging its way towards the plate.

Joe started laughing, didn't swing, and immediately grabbed the ball and looked at it. He was looking for something, anything. It might be tar, spit, tape, tobacco juice, gum, dots, gummy bears, or plutonium. Something was making the ball do things Joe had never seen before. But there was nothing on the ball. Joe smiled and insisted on another offering. And so Quentin did. He cranked it up again and again. Joe swung and missed, again and again. Missing and laughing, the Japanese all-star swore in disbelief.

It was the end of spring training for Tokyo Joe and also for Quentin Pugh. Pugh was unhittable. Unhittable and fat, but none of that seemed to matter now. It would only be a matter of time before the phone would ring. He headed home, to relax and think about eating a Ho Ho.

Mike Veeck of the St. Paul Saints called the next day. The Saints were a minor league team that was in the business of making baseball entertaining. Veeck's father Bill made history in baseball when he hired a midget to pinch hit in a real American League game, and his son was carrying on as a baseball entrepreneur.

Mike Veeck saw that Quentin would soon be a media star. A sumo wrestler who could pitch. He promptly signed Quentin, and his first outing was against the Sioux Falls Canaries.

For the game, Veeck had arranged to have a farm equipment company modify a small tractor to take Quentin out to the mound each inning. He had redesigned a device that would accommodate his weight while pitching. Defense would just not be a part of the plan. Batting would be out of the question, so the coach would have a designated hitter. Quentin rode out to the mound in his special Pope Mobile. The Pugh Mobile, he thought, as he came to a stop.

The umpire called batter up and then took the game ball from the pouch of the Saints new pig ball carrier. The pig's name was Bud Squeelie. Quentin thought the pig was a bit over the top for a baseball game but the fans seemed to love it.

The first Canary batter was a seven footer named Gaba who had emigrated from Somalia and took to baseball. Gaba's was a strike zone that Quentin knew he could hit. It would be three straight googlies. That's all he knew how to throw. He ended the inning with 12 pitches. Three strikeouts and that was the story, inning after inning. Only three balls were hit, and they resulted in two errors, so Quentin ended up winning the game 2 to 1. Quentin Pugh was on his way to stardom.

At the end of the game he tried to move into the dugout to relax. He was sitting down enjoying his new success when he looked down the bench and saw the team scorekeeper. She was beautiful. Her hair was tied back in a short ponytail that stuck out the back of her baseball hat. Her skin was soft and graced with natural blush. Hundreds of years ago women like her must have been the reason makeup was invented. Most of the players did not treat her like the beauty that she was because her father owned the team. Her name was on the back of her jersey: *Casey.*

Casey came down and put her hand out. She introduced herself as Casey Veeck. Quentin couldn't get his mouth to work. All he could come up with was a grunt and a sigh. She smiled and walked out of the dugout and onto the field. Quentin's eyes followed her. She was Aphrodite. She was delicious! Delicious was a word that he knew. Was this baseball or love? Was there a difference?

In everyone's life there is a moment of clarity and vision. Paul on the road to Damascus. Churchill's finest hour speech. The Babe's called shot in the fifth inning in 1932. Quentin was poised for such a moment. But for him it would be love. A love that would transport him from transient, heartless junk food love to true, indestructible diamond love.

Quentin was up against the Duluth Moonbeams. It was a day game and significant because there was to be an eclipse of the sun at two in the afternoon. Mike Veeck had a special event planned. Every customer got dark glasses to watch the eclipse.

At 1:55 the sun began to fade. Quentin was on the mound. He could see his shadow spilling in front of him. The shadow fell right where his foot would land on a pitch. His shadow was colossal. As the sun moved towards total eclipse he noticed that his shadow began to change its form. It began to shrivel. It was at the height of the eclipse that Quentin was able to see half the man he could be. He realized that if he was to know life and love, he had to be half a man. He knew it would happen because it was supposed to happen. Just as the eclipse is a part of the cycle of time. Quentin began to shrink.

After the game Quentin asked Casey if she could spare a few moments. She agreed and sat down next to him on the far end of the bench. They began talking and laughing. The other players glanced at them as they gathered gloves and bats. They knew Casey from previous seasons. They knew that she too knew obesity.

Quentin had heard that Casey had gone through a massive weight loss, and he asked her if she would be his coach. Not his girlfriend but his trainer. It was going to be a hard road, but Quentin knew that if he wanted to win his love he had to lose the weight.

Casey started him on a regimen that she had learned from her cousin in the Marine Corps. Cabbage soup and coffee. After a few weeks of the strong-smelling soup and caffeine jitters, Quentin was able to start moving.

Moving and walking with Casey was amazing for Quentin for multiple reasons. Unfortunately as he walked and lost weight, he began walking batters. Veeck noticed that the gyro was losing some of its googly, but he also knew that his star attraction was losing weight.

The weight loss tandem agreed to press on with physical workouts and a change in diet. The goal was set and so was the relationship. It wasn't long before the whole team knew that Casey and Quentin were an item. Casey and the Big Q didn't know they were in love. Everyone else could see it in them, but they couldn't see it in themselves.

The weight became their common goal. They started walking together and doing light workouts in the weight room. The Big Q had to move slowly and take care of his knees. It wasn't long, and he didn't need the little tractor to move out to the mound each inning. The pounds were coming off, and the opposing teams' batters were starting to hit the googly a bit more. Quentin countered by adding a knuckle ball to his pitch bag. The Saints, in an act that could only be thought of as humanitarian, were hitting over .400 when Quentin was pitching. It was their subconscious effort to help the love affair grow. Sentimental ballplayers were not the norm, but then the situation was special.

One day while Casey was keeping score, a foul ball came whistling into the dugout. The ball was headed for Casey's head. Quentin stabbed at the ball and deflected it. The rest of the players gasped. They had never seen Quentin move with such speed. He had taken the hit on his glove hand, so it wouldn't affect his pitching.

Casey thanked him knowing that he had probably saved her life. He joked and told her it was the cabbage soup. He took the ball and autographed it: *Casey, I love you, and I am always at bat for you.*

Casey read the ball and began to smile. One of those smiles that breaks into soft and dainty tears. Tears that only Quentin could see. The tears led to the laughing. The laughing led to the longer and longer walks. The walks led to the more and more pounds shed and eventually the proposal.

The "yes" led to the biggest marriage in Saints history as Mike Veeck's daughter and Quentin Pugh were married at home plate in St. Paul.

The sumo pitcher was no more. The loss of weight killed his pitch. He couldn't throw slow enough, and he couldn't master any other pitches. His career was over, but his life was back.

Casey and Quentin became special promotions organizers for the Saints. They worked to come up with crazy gimmicks to entertain fans. It was an odd run for baseball, but still a wonderful one because baseball, like all sports, takes to dramatic comeback stories, and theirs hit all the big themes. Unusual Success. Overcoming Adversity. Love.

Their first successful promo was diet night. Everyone in attendance who wished could get on the scale, and if they came back in two weeks and hit their goal weight they would get a prize. A collectible, limited edition, non-action figure of the 400 pound former great pitcher for the St. Paul Saints, Quentin Pugh.

The Uniques

Coach Greg Olson was an amateur baseball historian. He loved history, and the more obscure, the better. For him, it was all about fascinating tales. He was forever seeking information about events that were out of history books.

When he was young, he became interested in American slaves. At age eleven he surprised everyone when he read *Diary of an American Slave* by Frederick Douglas. Little Greg Olson was probably the only kid in Idaho who wrote a book report on a slave.

Growing up in Idaho didn't make history very diverse. The kids were told about cherry trees being cut down and Paul Revere's ride and Honest Abe's top hat. Though the young Greg did take a liking to Jefferson and Franklin, his teacher, Mrs. Lenten, didn't want him reading anything about Jefferson not freeing his slaves or the fact that he had a slave girlfriend named Sally.

"Mr. Olson, we are concentrating on Ben Franklin and Thomas Jefferson and their contributions to America and nothing else," Mrs. Lenten said sternly to him one day.

The "nothing else" of the forefathers was too provocative for grade school. Much like Leviticus in a Bible study, Idaho was not the place for dicey sexual stuff. This was how

Greg became a closet historian most of the time. Except for baseball history. Everyone knew that baseball was America's game and therefore, as pure as Idaho mountain snow.

Greg Olson had spent his entire life in Emmett, Idaho, a quiet, friendly town. He worked as an insurance agent. His son and daughter were happy in life and in play. His wife Kathy was a triathlete, which meant that he was in a kayak next to her when she swam, on a bike beside her when she did 15 mile training runs, and behind her when she was biking 30 miles. When he was done encouraging his wife he moved on to pitching batting practice to his son and daughter. He was their coach for all seasons.

He would switch assignments each year. One year he would coach his daughter's team and the next year his son's. The rest of his time he would help his wife train. If he wasn't on the ball field he was feeding Gatorade to his partner. His was a life of "atta boys." His coaching rotation in the new year would be his son's baseball team.

"Okay, boys, now listen up," Coach Olson said with an affirmative voice to his spring recruits. The newly-formed group of twelve year olds were wiggling with excitement at the beginning of a new season.

"We are a new team this year, and so I have a new name for our team," Greg began. The boys were paying close attention. They liked their coach. Greg Olson believed that the key to coaching was to have competitive practices, so he had devised a way of having the practice simulate real games. The kids loved it because it meant no one was on the bench, and the talent was more or less equal.

He was famous for unusual practices. One spring he set up a pitching machine and had it pointed to deep centerfield. He tried to recreate Willie Mays famous "the catch" at the Polo grounds. The young players couldn't do it, but they loved trying to run 514 feet to catch the ball. Each year they were ready to try and catch the ball. Olson would laugh at their efforts, yelling, "Now, don't forget! If you do catch it, then you have to turn and throw it to second base."

The kids marveled at his baseball knowledge about an event that happened thirty years before they were born and were always waiting for the new surprises.

The wigglers stopped moving for the coach's big preseason speech. Olson, in a commanding voice, began, "This year our team is going to be called the Bucks, after Buck O'Neill, an old black baseball player that died recently."

"The Bucks? That's a strange name for a team," the team's smart kid said. "Why can't we be the Einsteins? That's a cool name".

"You're right. That is a cool name," Greg said. "But Einstein himself would have said that it's all relative," he said with a wink to the smart kid. "No," he continued. "This year we are going to be The Bucks. The beauty of this name is that you young hunters can think of deer if it helps you remember it."

The kids nodded in approval.

"At least we're not *The Does*," one of the players shouted. The rest of the players got a big kick out of that.

"Yeah, but bucks get shot" another responded. All of the kids were laughing now.

The coach laughed too and continued, "So, The Bucks we are, and next week I will tell you a little about Buck O'Neill of the Kansas City Monarchs."

The week passed and Greg's son Jeremy was very curious.

"C'mon, Dad, can't you tell me more about this Buck O'Neill?

Greg paused. "No," he said. "Not until we are all together. Maybe you want to pick up his book on the coffee table there. At the next practice throw something in about him."

Jeremy grabbed the book and retreated to his room.

At the next practice, Greg was ready.

"Alright, Bucks, it's time to go!" he shouted. "Let's stretch and warm up with a slow jog."

"What about the name of our team?" Jeremy queried.

"*You* read the book, Jeremy," his father said, with a hint of pride. "*You* tell them."

Jeremy looked around at his teammates for a moment and then spoke.

"Buck O'Neill was a fabulous player who played for the Kansas City Monarchs of the Negro Leagues."

"What's a negro, Coach?" Mike the first baseman asked.

"An African American, Mike. In the old days they wouldn't allow black people and white people to play ball together."

"That's kind of stupid if you ask me," a freckled-faced boy replied. "I mean, how could they do that?"

Jeremy stepped in again. "Some black players pretended they were Cuban, and then for some reason they could play. Right, Dad?"

"That's right, Jeremy," Greg said. "It was a strange time in history. I'll tell you more about it tomorrow, but for now let's run some laps."

The kids groaned and set off on their way. One, the Vogel kid, stayed behind.

"Is everything alright, Bill?" Greg asked.

"Yeah, I'm okay, I guess," the kid said. "It's just that my dad is kind of confused about this name. Are we named after deer or what?"

"Don't worry, Bill," Greg said. "I'll call him tonight and explain."

Later that day the Olson family sat down for dinner. At least one night a week the family would do something together. The phone rang, and Kathy Olson answered it.

"Oh, hello, Mr. Vogel. How are you?" she said. "Yes, he's here." She handed Greg the phone.

"Yes, Mr. Vogel, I was going to give you a call"

Dan Vogel came out swinging.

"Listen here, Olson!" he said in an irate voice. "I don't want no kid of mine playing on team named after a nigger."

"I beg your pardon," Greg said in shock. "What did you just say?"

"You heard me," Vogel snapped back.

Greg was speechless.

"Listen, Mr. Vogel," Greg began. "That kind of language could get you in a lot of trouble, and I certainly hope you don't use it often. As far as the team name goes, that's our team's business, not yours." He paused in an effort to calm himself. "However, I'm not going to let a team name get in the way of a kid playing baseball, so I will change the name. I don't want you to mention our conversation to your son. I want him to think about baseball."

Vogel grunted on the other end of the line, "Well, I suppose I wasn't being all PC or something."

Olson working to diffuse the situation spoke fast, "Let's move on, Dan. Buck O'Neill would want baseball to win out, so we will have a new name by tomorrow. An original name for a bunch of original kids. But remember—nothing of this to your son. I don't want him in this at all. He is a player, not someone who has to worry about language."

"Yeah, sure, no more about it then. Sorry about the—" Vogel paused. "—the language."

"Who was that?" Olson's wife asked.

"That was Billy Vogel's white separatist father who—and I quote—'don't want a son of his on a team named after an n-word.'"

"Really, I didn't think those folks were around here anymore. I thought they moved to Montana or somewhere."

"Well, I guess they are still here," Olson said, shaking his head in disgust.

"I think Vogel is tying to reform," Kathy said. "His first wife died. I think he married that nice Smith lady, the Mormon, who owns the laundry service."

"Yeah, that would work," Greg muttered. "He probably gets his white hooded sheets starched to a crisp there."

"Greg, now stop that!" Kathy said. "She is a nice lady. I know she is not prejudiced."

"I know, but it was pretty bizarre," he said. "I am a student of history, and I thought that stuff was . . ."

"Was what?"

"History!"

Kathy smiled sympathetically at him.

"So what are you going to do about the team name?" she asked.

"I'm going to change it. I'd rather think more about baseball and less about racial issues."

"Good idea," she replied. "So what is the team name going to be?"

"Our new name will be The Uniques," he said. "Like it?"

Kathy smiled. "Sounds perfect. Where did you get the idea?"

Greg smiled back at her, but there was a glint of sneakiness in his eyes.

"Funny you should ask. It's the name of a Negro Baseball team from Brooklyn that played in 1868."

"Is that going to be a problem with Vogel?"

"Nope," Greg replied. "White separatists don't know anything about anyone who isn't white. Didn't you know?"

Olson looked at him fondly and gave him a slight embrace.

"I know The Uniques have a coach that is one-of-a-kind."

Our Lady of Centerfield

Juan Diego was familiar with all of the legends of the Mayan. He lived and played baseball in a small village on the Yucatan peninsula, the home of the ancient Mayan ruins of Chichen Itza.

He and his family would make a pilgrimage to the Mayan temple each year on the 21st of March, the vernal equinox. His children loved the day. They loved being a part of the thirty thousand people watching the shadow. "Papa! The snake, look! The snake is coming!" the children would whisper respectfully.

At sunset, a glowing ray of yellow would appear on the temple's celestial stairs. A shadow would appear on the back of the holy snakes that decorated the steps. The serpent was sacred to the Mayan people. The shadow would move down the snake and settle on the ground.

The ancient Mayans used the sign as a signal to plant. The snake was their calendar for a thousand years. But Juan Diego's children didn't care about planting time. They loved the magic.

The Mayan magic came to Juan's village one spring. It was a year that the peasants would remember and tell stories about. A moment when the village priest would understand the power of the ancients.

The memory of the Virgin Mother's appearance in centerfield was a part of Juan's story. A baseball tale as full of wonder and magic as the ruins of the Mayan's. Why it happened and how it happened doesn't seem to matter. The people of the village didn't care. The Virgin came, and it was good.

The months leading up to the baseball season were hard. Old people were dying and many children were sick. The Ministry of Health didn't have any idea what had infected the village, and no one could stop the mystery epidemic. The priest did as much as he could to soothe his flock, but there was no cure.

Baseball doesn't cure disease, but it did offer the town relief from their misery. The fact that Juan and his team were winning was a form of grace. Though the priest hated to admit it, the local team did more for the spirits of the people than the church. Juan's team had only one loss all spring, and that was to the team from tiny San Francisco.

The lesser known San Francisco of Mexico was about five kilometers away from Juan's village. They were so close they shared the same priest. San Francisco had beaten Juan's team easily, with their famous left-handed pitcher. There didn't appear to be much hope of defeating the plague or San Francisco.

On the day of the big game, Juan was in centerfield in front of a huge Corona beer sign. He was the best player in the province. "Don't hit it to center. It's a black hole out there," everyone in his dugout prayed.

The date for the game was March 21st, the same day as the celebration at the pyramid. Juan's family passed on their trip to the ruins to watch their father play baseball. Baseball was as sacred to them as the ceremony was to their ancestors.

Juan's family could see the sun drop towards the rain forest behind their father. The sun was low in the sky like it would be at the Mayan ruin. Juan could feel the sun on his back. It was close to the tree tops, and the shadows on the field were long and ghostlike. Juan didn't notice, he just kept catching balls and throwing people out.

With the score 4 to 3 in favor of his team, Juan was concentrating on the batter. He had a routine. After each pitch he would reach down and grab a blade of grass. He would just pluck it and throw it up in the air. Over his shoulder he saw a glow on the sign behind him. He was nervous because he didn't want to miss a pitch, so he couldn't concentrate on what he saw. His teammate in leftfield yelled, "Juan, look behind you."

With both Juan and the leftfielder distracted, their coach called a time out. He was trying to get his players back in the game. His message went unheeded. There were no longer baseball players in the field. There were penitents, true believers. Juan was on his knees as were all the other players. On the Corona beer sign, for all to see, was a vivid glowing image of the Blessed Virgin Mary.

It was Mexico, it was baseball, and it was a miracle. There was no hysteria. Even those who had not been to Mass in 20 years could see the beauty of the Lady.

The game stopped, and the fans came walking ever so slowly onto the field. They moved reverently so as not to scare the image away. One of the bat boys ran across the street to get the priest. The priest left Mass and came running to the diamond. The Mass and the game had stopped.

Father Gonzales approached Juan.

"What happened? What did you do?" he asked.

"I did nothing, Father," Juan said. "Except catch fly balls, and I do that every Saturday."

"Juan, this is truly a special day," the priest murmured. "We must pray now."

With that, Father took out his rosary. "Let us pray," he said. "Let us begin with the Joyful Mysteries."

And so they did, baseball hats aside, beer cups put down, children quiet; the baseball game became a spiritual experience. As Father closed with the last Hail Mary the Virgin faded and went away. The crowd quietly went their way. Many went on to the church to receive confession or take communion.

The team from San Francisco left quietly. They gave their respects and said that they would be back again next year. They wished Juan and the rest of his teammates well and headed home with the vision in their heads.

Shortly after the appearance of the Virgin in Centerfield, the bad things went away. People were no longer sick. The children were back in school, the crops were being put in according to the snake legend. For many days after, the people came to the ballpark to see if the Virgin had returned, but she did not. The rumor throughout the province was that she would return the next year on the same day. It was a mystery.

March 21st of the following year, the vernal equinox and baseball were back. The believers thought it was a good idea to repeat the events. Some thought that perhaps Our Lady cared for baseball. The bishop, who had made a special trip for the game, told the people to pray the rosary and to forget these foolish notions that Jesus's mother liked baseball.

The game was scheduled against San Francisco out of respect for their players and fans. The people of San Francisco shared the miracle, and they came. The entire town was there. Sitting, waiting, and praying. The sun began to go down in the 4th inning much like it had the previous year. Juan was in the batter's box. With the score 3 to 3, Juan's team desperately needed a run, and he hoped he could get it. He was not a homerun hitter. He was a contact hitter. He batted for average like Joe DiMaggio and Rod Carew. He knew he had to change his stroke.

The next pitch brought the grace. Juan hit it solidly over the bright Corona sign in centerfield. The crowd forgot about the apparition. No more pilgrimages—this was baseball time. Even the bishop was on his feet. The boys on the scoreboard fought off the glare of the sun to register the big white four, which hung on the hook and swung from side to side in celebration. At precisely that moment the sun hit the gaping hole in the score board, blessing both the 4 and the 3.

After Jaun made is his trip around the bases, he sat down and told his teammate that the score was now the same as last year when the mother appeared. Juan could see the San Francisco centerfielder was staring at the sign where she had appeared. He could hear the buzz of the crowd and then the movement on the bleachers as the fans were getting on their knees. Even the skeptical bishop was on his knees. He had made a special trip to rebuke the story of the baseball Virgin. Now seeing the miracle himself he ran on the field with his rosary.

"My children, please join me in the rosary, quick, so Our Lady can hear us," the bishop entreated. As the bishop was saying the mysteries, Juan noticed the scorekeepers were moving about on the scoreboard. He also noticed that when they moved, it cast shadows on the Lady. It was like the shadows he had seen at Chichen Itza.

The young boys on the scoreboard stood side by side, and the vision disappeared. Juan interrupted the bishop and yelled up to boys, "Please sit down for a moment." They did, and the Bishop started praying again.

"Your Excellency," Juan said. "I'm afraid the image is being caused by the sun coming through the scoreboard. It is only an illusion of light."

The bishop stood up in a huff and glared disapproval towards Juan and the boys as if they had fooled him.

"Your Excellency, it doesn't make the vision any less miraculous," Juan told him. "Our Lady cured the village. She appeared with the spring sun like the Mayans."

"Don't talk to me of Mayans," the Bishop spat. "This is blasphemy!" He turned to his subordinate priest. "Father, come with me and tell your parishioners they belong in mass, not on this green grass in the sun. Get back to church! All of you."

Juan and the others were discouraged. The crowd got up reluctantly and began filing out. Some, with their heads bowed, moved on to Mass. The others walked silently to their homes. The faithful knew something happened, something miraculous. The people stopped dying, the children were healthy and the crops were rich. The believers knew, deep in their Mayan hearts, that Our Lady loved them, and she also loved baseball.

The Effey Mosquitoes

Juan didn't much care for mosquitoes. In the Dominican Republic, he had seen mosquitoes, but not the size of the ones in Northern Minnesota. It was not that they were inherently bad but catching a baseball while trying to ward off hoards of blood-sucking insects the size of air buses was daunting.

The name of his team was the Effey Mosquitoes. That and the fact that the town square had a Paul Bunyan sized statue of a mosquito should have been a sign.

Juan was near tears trying to swat them off while concentrating on the batters at the plate. His only break would come when the Walker Lumberjacks gorilla of a lefty would come up to bat. When the monster pull hitter stepped into the box, Juan could swat and twist and work full time to protect himself. He would wait until the cleanup hitter stepped up to the plate and then start slapping the mosquitoes on his ankles.

Juan had been introduced to DEET in early June, but it didn't seem to affect these behemoths of the north. His was a hell like no others.

"How bad is it?" questioned Margie as Juan stepped into the dugout after the final out of the inning.

"Oh my God. It is hell out there," the welt-ridden Juan replied.

Margie, the bat girl for the Effey team and the daughter of the coach, had noticed how uncomfortable he was in leftfield.

Juan was Margie's friend and mentor. She wanted to be a Spanish teacher and Juan was her ticket to fluency. She had met him at language camp. When she came home she told her dad that she had met a Dominican at camp. Her father immediately set in motion an effort to bring Juan to his contending team. Reluctantly, Margie relayed the bad news: that Juan couldn't hit curveballs.

"Margie, he's a Dominican," her father said. "Just that is enough. I don't care if he can hit curveballs. The people from the Dominica Republic are not very good at skiing, but they can play baseball. A bad Dominican baseball player is an all-star in Minnesota."

Juan finally agreed to a contract and came to Margie's hometown for the summer. He was staying with Margie's uncle, the town sheriff, and so far was enjoying his stay. It gave him a chance to practice his English and to better understand the American culture. What he didn't appreciate were the mosquitoes.

In an effort to understand the nature of the insects, Juan did a crash course in entomology. He learned that it's only the female mosquitoes that bite and that they use the blood for nurturing their eggs. None of this helped him. Leftfield was torture.

The true crisis surfaced when the Effey Mosquitoes were in a close game with their rivals, the Walker Lumberjacks, and the pests wouldn't leave him alone.

The top of the ninth inning came with his team ahead by one run. The Lumberjacks had a man on second with two outs. One more out to save the game. While Juan was busy in left swatting, the Lumberjacks slugger was waiting.

The Mosquitoes pitcher threw his fast ball, but it was not fast enough because as fast as it came in, it was sent out in the field even faster. Right in the direction of Juan and his little "friends." The ball was hit high, and there was plenty of room and time for Juan to move under it. Unfortunately the bugs in left used the extra time to call in a squadron, and they attacked Juan with a vengeance.

Juan was covered in mosquitoes. They were at his ankles, in his hair, in his ears and worst of all in his eyes. The ball came straight down and caromed off his noggin and over the short leftfield fence for a homerun.

Margie had seen enough. She waited until after the game to console him and to also to share her plan. Her plan was a unique one, but she had a feeling it would bring relief.

"Tough break out there," Margie consoled Juan. "But I think I can help."

Juan looked up at her, suddenly interested.

"Listen, games are not won or lost on one play," Margie continued. "If Sullivan wouldn't have been thrown out at third, we'd probably still be batting. It's not your fault. However, we need to get rid of those critters in leftfield."

"You have a good idea, Margie?" Juan said in his lovable broken English.

"Yes, I do," she told him. "Tomorrow morning, go to the hardware store and tell them you want to catch a butterfly."

Juan looked at her as if she were loco and said "And what is butterfly and why do I want to catch?"

"Don't worry about that," Margie replied. "Just get a butterfly net and come over to my house, okay?"

"Okay." Juan smiled. His bright white smile made him everyone's favorite player. Including the winged devils in left.

Juan followed Margie's instructions to the letter. At nine the next morning, he was at her house, butterfly net still with the price tag hanging on it.

"*¿Estàs listo?*" Margie said with enthusiasm.

"*Sí*, Margie," he said, holding up the net. "I am ready."

"Have you ever been in a canoe?" she asked. He looked at her puzzled for a minute.

Margie thought for a second, "*¿Como un barco? ¿Canoa?*"

"But why?"

"Do you want to get rid of the bugs or not?"

"Yes, I do," Juan affirmed.

Twenty minutes later, after hauling the canoe a few blocks, they stood on the muddy bank of the local pond.

"You take the front, Juan, "Margie said pointing. "I'll steer, you just paddle."

Juan got in and nearly fell into the water, but Margie steadied the boat.

"Is very far?" Juan asked nervously.

"Not far," she assured him. "Just paddle on that side. See those trees ahead? That's where we are headed."

"You are good at this," Juan said.

"I should be—I taught canoeing at camp. Okay, I'll steer us in, just pull your paddle out as we approach the shore. And grab your net."

Juan, with his net in hand looked puzzled,

"What are we going to do?" Then he screamed. "What are those?"

"'Those are our leftfield defense," Margie answered.

Juan wasn't convinced.

"Dragonflies," Margie explained. "They are your saviors. *Los salvadores*?" She netted a dozen dragonflies in one swoop.

"Dragonflies—do they bite?" "They do, but not people. Only mosquitoes," Margie told him happily.

She began emptying the net into a large cardboard box that was covered with fine gauze. Assured that these new bugs wouldn't bite him, Juan had a turn at scooping them up.

"We are going to take dragonflies to the ball field?"

"Yes, that's the plan," Margie said. "Then they will eat all those mosquitoes that have been biting you. *¿Buena idea, no?*"

Juan stated laughing, invigorated at the thought of fighting back.

"If this takes care of those devils, I will stay here all day." Juan stated confidently.

"It shouldn't take too long," Margie said. "We'll get a few more in the box, and then tomorrow we release them at game time."

"Margie, I hope this works."

The chance to go to state was Margie's fathers dream and since it was she who had brought Juan to town, she wanted to make sure everyone saw him shine.

Before the game, Margie dragged the dragon box along the foul line and out into Juan's territory. The crowd had begun to gather in the stands. Juan ran out to his position past Margie.

He gave her a big smile, "Are you going to release them now?"

"Do you think I should?" she asked.

"Why not?"

Margie smiled back and pulled the gauze off the top of the box, giving a thousand perplexed dragonflies their buffet ticket. Juan was ecstatic. He could see them, a great flying crowd, and heard them eating the skeeters immediately.

Fly ball after fly ball came his way, and Juan caught all of them. The wild crowd of Effey fans were nodding their heads in unison and yelling to Margie, "She's our girl! Margie is our MVP!" Margie's father gave her a big hug as his team mounted a huge inning and drove the Lumberjacks pitcher out of the game.

Juan for his part went four for four with a homerun. He hit a curveball 400 feet and yelled "curveball" to Margie as he came around third.

"I knew you could hit one," she yelled, and the crowd applauded in agreement.

Juan and a teammate raised Margie onto their shoulders at end of the game. "We are off to the championship in St. Paul, Margie!"

"Yes, we are," Margie giggled. "And the only Mosquitoes going are us."

The Cleveland Indian Indian

The fact that Isaac Fox Eagle from Standing Rock Reservation was the rightfielder for the Cleveland Indians should have been in the News of the Weird section of the newspaper.

Ben Two Feather, age eleven, knew it wasn't weird because he had Isaac's rookie baseball card. If you got the card you knew it was true. Ben saw him on TV, but he didn't believe it. The team being called the Indians sort of threw him. He wasn't sure if Isaac was a real player or if they were using him like one of those cigar store Indians at Wall Drug in South Dakota.

When you're an Indian kid on the rez you expect disappointment. If you're not expecting promises to be broken, you're a fool. Ben and Isaac were not easily fooled because they both were descendents of Sitting Bull. Real descendents, not like the people up in Fort Yates.

The Indians at Fort Yates said they had Sitting Bull's body, but Ben and his family knew that he was buried near Little Eagle. Isaac and the rest of the village kept it a secret because they didn't want the white people to come and dig him up and take him to the fancy museum out in Washington D.C. Sitting Bull's people were afraid they would take him away like they did the buffalo and the Black Hills and the casinos.

Ben's friend Walter would say, "Hey Ben, have you heard about the new white wine."

"No, what is it?"

Walter would giggle and say in a high voice, "We want a casino!"

Ben would laugh and reply, "Yeah that's the way it is Walter, but we have Isaac Fox Eagle, and he's on a real baseball card."

At home in the trailer or "the factory manufactured home" as his mother insisted it should be called, she was waiting for him.

"Have you heard the good news, Ben?"

She was a handsome woman. She was not movie star beautiful but kind of a handsome beautiful. She was the prairie. Her face shined like sweet grass.

"What are you talking about mother?" Ben teased. "Sometimes you speak in riddles like Walter."

"Oh yes, Mr. Smarty pants. Here is a Walter riddle. What boy is going on a bus to Minneapolis to see Isaac Fox Eagle and the Cleveland Indians?"

Ben just about wet his pants. It was true; he and many others from the rez were going to be sitting in rightfield behind the Indian on the Indians.

Isaac Fox Eagle was tearing up the league, and that's why he could take a risk and have his tribal brothers and sisters come to the game. He paid for their tickets with his bonus and with 20 homeruns in the young season he was going to be a big star.

The bus trip was long, but it didn't matter to Ben Two Feather and his friends.

"Hey, Ben," it was Walter, the Heyoka, speaking. Heyoka was the Lakota word for spiritual clown. The Indian clown was respected. Everyone knew that Walter's humor had a message. "Did you hear about the white man who went to the psychiatrist and started yelling 'I'm a teepee. I'm a wigwam . . .' the Indian doctor told him he was too tents".

All of the kids on the bus groaned except one kid named Red Cloud. Somebody had to explain it to him for 50 miles.

The kids were elated. Several years earlier they were suppose to go to Minnesota for a basketball tournament, but the funding fell through. This time nothing was going to be taken from the Hunk Papa, Sitting Bull's clan. This time no "Indian giving." Ben had a plan.

"Hey Ben, what's with the first baseman's glove? You play rightfield." A kid quipped.

"I am going to catch a homerun hit by the greatest Indian ball player of all time. And then when he is in the Hall of Fame they will call me and say 'hey can we have that ball?' and I'm going to say 'no!' And then I'm going to bury it near Sitting Bull, and they won't be able to get it ever."

Most of the kids gave Ben the "whatever" look. Only Walter understood his words.

The game couldn't get started fast enough for the kids. As soon as they cleared the turnstiles they rushed to the concession stands. Some were buying Cleveland hats, and others were buying expensive food. One of the girls asked if they sold fry bread. They all laughed and teased the girl and said "only in Cleveland."

Ben was in line waiting patiently for his Dome dog. A young college kid in a green Twins hat was standing behind him.

He smiled at Ben and started up a conversation, "Hey, are you with the group from South Dakota?"

"Yes, I am. Are you a Twins fan?" Ben knew that the Twins colors were blue and red, so he was confused. "I noticed that you have a green Twins hat."

"Yeah, I looked all over for it. They're new. Look here. It's got a shamrock on the back. It's an Irish American thing. My name is Hoolihan. What's yours?"

"My name is Ben. The Irish are proud people, huh?" Ben said trying to act older.

"How about you? Are you a Cleveland Indian fan or a fan of your friend from the reservation?"

Ben thought for a moment. It was like a trick question. "Oh. I guess I'm a fan of Isaac Fox Eagle."

"Listen, Ben, I'm sitting in the same section as you guys today, so I'm going to be an Isaac Fox Eagle fan, too. Is that cool? Is his rookie card out yet?"

"Oh yes! I already have two of them, and you know what else?"

"What?" the young man with the Irish hat asked.

"I'm going to catch Isaac's homerun ball," Ben said excitedly.

"Good for you. I'm with you, man. I'll be watching. Later, dude." The young man walked away with his afternoon eats.

Ben headed to his seat with his Dome dog in hand. The rest of the kids were already there. Ben was in an aisle seat, which would make his homerun ball catching easier. He looked for the guy with the funny green Twins hat, but he couldn't see him.

"Playball was the call," and in unison the entire section from Little Eagle yelled, "Hoka Hey," which meant "let's get going." The white kids around them thought they were going to attack. The only one attacking would be Isaac, the superstar baseball player from Little Eagle.

He doubled in the first inning, and when he came out to his position he tipped his hat with the logo of the Indian with the big nose. Ben thought maybe it was an Indian from the Cleveland area because he had never seen a prairie Indian with a nose like the one on the hat. The kids were screaming at the sight of their hometown hero.

Fox Eagle was no surprise. He had been a batting champ in college at the University of Nebraska, and he went high in the draft. All America watched to see what would happen if he was drafted first by the Cleveland Indians. Would he sign? Did the team name offend him? Would they change the name? What would he do?

He signed for almost a million dollars and built a community center in Little Eagle and another one in Fort Yates. He was very generous. Ben's mother said he was a "philanthropist." Ben thought it was a really big word for kind.

Isaac was a bigger legend then Sitting Bull to the young people. He hit monster homeruns right up to the thunder beings in the sky. The elders thought his balls were causing rain clouds. There were stories on the rez that he hit a homerun that flew over the Missouri river ten miles away. Ben didn't believe that one.

Deep into the game Ben looked up at the scoreboard and saw that the Indians were down by one run, and Isaac was up next. All of the kids were anxious. They wanted Isaac to do well, but they were in the Twins stadium. They didn't want to start any trouble.

"After all, we are outnumbered," Walter joked.

"This ain't no Little Big Horn," Ben assured them that it was baseball not Custer's Last Stand.

The 6' 6" Indian stepped into the box. He tapped his spikes four times for the four directions and readied himself to send a message to the thunder beings. Isaac knew the traditional way. The thunder beings were in the clouds.

The Twins pitcher was nicknamed Mephistopheles because he allegedly threw fire. He wound up and hurled a fire ball. Fox Eagle swung and put out the flame with a blast of wood that sent the ball flying to right.

Ben saw the ball come off the bat. It was as big as a beach ball, and he could see that it was flying to section 114, row 17, and seat 38. His seat.

There was a big fat college kid in front of him, but Ben had the big snare glove. He held up his glove and looked into it, and the ball was already embedded in the web as if it had come from the factory that way.

Everyone was excited for Ben. The Twins fans on the other hand were not Indians or Indian fans, so they were not happy.

"Throw it back. Throw it back," came the chant.

"Walter, what are they saying?"

"They want you to throw it back to taunt the other team. It's some stupid thing the Cubs fans started. That's all they can do in Chicago."

"I'm not throwing it back," Ben said stoically, in the true Lakota way.

The shouting got louder and louder and some of the girls in the group were getting anxious.

"Ben, just throw it back. We will buy you a stupid ball."

"No, I say no. It has to stop somewhere. We need to take a stand."

"Easy there, Ben," Walter counseled. "This isn't a treaty deal. It's a baseball game."

"Not just any baseball. This one was hit by a Lakota chief."

The pressure was mounting. Ben was near tears. Some of the older boys who were Twins fans were looking at Ben. It was going to be a long bus ride back to the rez if Ben didn't surrender.

He looked at the ball. "Throw it back. Throw it back," was louder than the music in the stadium. He had no choice. He was fighting back the tears of another promise broken. Ben looked down at his opened hand. The Fox Eagle relic was looking up at him. One tear fell and landed on the ball. More tears were waiting when another hand grabbed the ball and put a dirty crusty one in its place. Ben looked up in shock.

"Hey, Ben." The voice belonged to the Irish guy with the green hat. "Not so fast. Throw the dirty one. These folks won't know the difference."

Ben didn't hesitate and threw the ball far onto the field, making sure he didn't hit the Twins rightfielder. He turned toward his new friend to thank him.

"Thanks!"

The two new friends had a collective laugh at the expense of the crowd and high fived each other. The Lakota nation did their famed war whoop, and the rest of the crowd exalted in a collective taunt of the visiting team, but Ben still had the "real" ball.

Ben turned toward the rest of the kids and smiled. His head moved up and down affirmingly like a bobbing head doll. The Indians had won.

The Sign of the Cross

Bob was an unusual name for a Panamanian. Though his last name, Rodriguez, was common enough in that part of the world. Bob was not an easy name for locals to pronounce. Half the time he was Bab, and the rest of the time he was Boob. Life was not easy for a Bob in a small fishing village in Central America.

He grew up in Porto Bello on the Caribbean. The village was known throughout Panama for its fresh fish and Black Jesus. The legendary Black Jesus was a statue in the church that had many stories attributed to it. Bob was one of the stories.

Bob had learned that his father was an American serviceman who served in the Canal Zone. Like many American servicemen throughout the years, his father had a girlfriend, who, after he went home to the USA, had a baby.

Bob wondered if his father was alive. Was he a Mormon? Did he have black hair? Did he play baseball? These were questions he had asked his mother but she didn't have many answers. She did know he was Catholic. Although she didn't marry him. It didn't matter. At least he was Catholic. Bob was Catholic, too. Bob was Panamanian, so Bob was Catholic. That's just the way it is in Panama.

He couldn't care less if his dad had been of the same religion. He wondered if his dad had played baseball, and if so, what position. Maybe he played for some minor league team. He doubted that he could still be playing, but he could hope. When Bob was a young boy, he would rifle though baseball cards to see if his dad was on one of them.

He would brag to his pals and tell them that he got his name from his dad and that his dad was a catcher, too, and that he might be in the majors. His teammates didn't care. They were just ball players.

"Well, let's hope he is faster than you," they would tease.

"Hey, I'm squatting like a duck for nine innings," Bob would counter.

Which made his teammates start quacking like a duck in Spanish.

"Do you guys think you could do this?" Bob would snap back sometimes, resorting to that old catcher gesture of handing them the mask. No one ever took it.

Bob didn't speak English. He thought it might come later, genetically, like heart disease. After all, he was half American. His dream was to play professional baseball in America. At night, he would look for games on TV. He would watch the major league players and get tips on how to hold his bat and tilt his hat. But never sideways—he hated that look. Especially when pitchers did it. He was convinced that they threw worse if their hats were crooked.

He loved the little mannerisms of the big league players, especially the Latino players. He noticed that all the Latino players would make the sign of the cross before batting. Bob thought it looked pretty cool, and whenever he had a chance he would make the Father, Son and Holy Ghost sign on his head and chest. Many people in Panama would make the sign of the cross whenever they walked by a church or a cemetery. Bob remembered the old lady who used to walk the streets in his neighborhood, crossing herself all the time. All the kids thought she was either really holy or really crazy. Bob wasn't crazy or holy, but he wanted results. He wanted hits. Not just hits. He wanted homeruns.

The gesture of making a cross on his chest fit Bob's routine. He had a regimental approach. On the night before the game he prayed to St. Ambrose to handle curveballs and to St. Michael to hit fastballs. Bob thought that the sign of the cross would be a good way to hit sliders. Hitting a baseball is only successful a third of the time, so he needed all the help he could get. He had the picture cards of the saints in his back pocket for good luck.

Colón was the name of the big city that was near Bob's town. Colón had a pitcher that was a giant left-hander. George Steinbrenner, the Yankee owner, was rumored to want him. The CIA was going to help kidnap this pitcher from the Colón team since the druglord owner wouldn't sell him. He was magnificent, like the statue in Porto Bello, and there were just as many fables about him. His fastball had been clocked at over 100 miles an hour. Bob would need some heavenly help.

Bob was the lead-off batter. His stomach was churning. He hoped he could just keep the contents from flying out onto the field. The umpire yelled, "Play ball!" and Bob started shaking. The sound that the ball made when it hit the catcher's mitt was like Indiana Jones whip. A sound barrier-breaking snap.

In his many years of baseball, Bob had never forgotten to make the sign of the cross. But on this day, his nerves jangled about the Colón pitcher, he simply forgot.

He was trying to focus on the ball as the rocket came toward him. Before he could even fathom high and inside, his helmet exploded. The ball, traveling 100 miles an hour, had sailed high and to the left right into his red helmet. The crowd groaned and someone yelled, "Call the mortuary!" The umpire leaned over him and shouted, "He's still alive. Get him to the hospital! Quick!"

Bob woke up that night to a strange vision. He was remembering his childhood in Porto Bello. The story of the Black Jesus and how it floated onto the shore. The Black Jesus had arrived just in time to save the people from the plague. Bob had a small statue of him in his locker. Now he was trying to figure out why the Black Jesus image was in his mind.

He sat up and tried to remember what had happened and why he was in a hospital bed. The door opened and there was a stream of light. Standing in silhouette was a huge man. Shadowy and dark, he had very long hair and was wearing a robe. Once Bob's eyes adjusted, he realized that the figure was the Black Jesus. The statue was not a statue on this night. The Black Jesus was moving, and it looked as if His lips were moving, too. The figure's very presence seemed to be saying, *Bob, I know you are a true believer, but you must understand that prayer is for wisdom and love not for hitting baseballs. You may pray with the sign of the cross, but please pray for your good will and for all those you love. Not for homeruns.*

Bob laid back in his hospital bed, struck with guilt. The Black Jesus had saved the people of Porto Bello, watching over them, listening to their prayers and worries. Now, Bob knew that there was a place for suspicion and a place for faith. He knew that his holy place was a diamond, ringed with splintery wooden bleachers and the smell of cheap beer. He thought of the Bible verse that instructed people to render unto Caesar that which is Caesar's. Or in this specific case, render unto to baseball what is baseball and to the Black Jesus what is His.

He would continue to pray to his patron saints, but the sign of the cross was an act of faith for safety. At every at-bat, Bob now would say, "In the name of the Father, the Son and the Holy Ghost. May God and the Black Jesus protect me from high inside fast balls. Amen."

The Schizophrenic Centerfielder

Terry and I were baseball Robin Hoods. We were going to steal something of value for the first time in our lives. It just happened to be a baseball. A very old baseball.

I picked up Terry at about 9 am. He was sitting on the front step smoking his pipe. I was too far away to smell his cherry blend tobacco, but I thought I could smell it. He looked ready to take on "the job." The mission was a criminal activity that both of us agreed had to be done.

Terry was one of the most fascinating people I had ever met. He was intelligent, creative, athletic, generous, loyal and schizophrenic. His mental disease did not seem to affect his everyday life, but then that was because he spent time with me. I have difficulty with reality myself, so I am hardly one to judge. He was quite ordinary looking: six feet tall and slender. He was in his sixties, had most of his hair and for the most part was in great shape. He looked like he could step up to the plate and hit a few singles. He had been a minor league player with a future, but his hallucinations and spells had put an end to aspirations.

The first time I met him was outside a coffee shop. It was July, and he was standing near his car wearing headphones.

"Is that good stuff you're listening to?" I asked. "I hope you don't mind me asking."

"I'm listening to Christmas carols," he replied with a friendly tone.

I could tell he was sincere. Although I had just met him, I could tell that he told the truth. Even if it was his "truth."

"Christmas carols in July," I said. "Isn't that kind of crazy?"

He laughed. "Yeah, you got that right. I am crazy. How about you?"

"Yeah, me, too," I added with a chuckle. "But why in July?"

"Good question," he said. "Well, the music is really good, and I find that if I listen to it out of season it says more to me and I enjoy it more."

"That makes sense," I allowed. "Nothing crazy about that."

This exchange began our friendship. At that time I didn't know that he was a diagnosed schizophrenic. Over the years we shared stories, insights and literature. We were men who liked to read. Men who liked baseball, a good book and a strong cup of coffee.

Terry was a talented writer, so we shared words as a vocation, but what we had most in common was baseball. And on this day it was one ball in particular. Babe Ruth had hit the ball out of Wrigley Field in Chicago in 1932. It was on display in a museum in Witro, Minnesota. Witro is a small town in southern Minnesota that got its name from Lakota Indians. The Plains tribes lived in the area until they were driven to casinos years ago. The word Witro means "crazy people."

The curators of the museum had decided to sell the ball. The Spaulding baseball they were selling was thought to be the ball that Ruth hit out of Wrigley Field. It was a famous homerun because "the Babe" predicted the homer by pointing his bat out to centerfield as a warning to the pitcher. The pitcher didn't heed the warning and Number 3 hit the ball 411 feet into the stands. Norwegian farmer Syd Larson and his brother Lars happened to be in the ball park that day, and Syd caught the ball. The two brothers were amateur historians in town touring the Chicago Natural History Museum. Years later Syd died when he was sucked into a combine. His bachelor brother gave the ball to the museum along with hundreds of Indian artifacts. One of the artifacts was part of General Custer's scalp from the Battle of Little Big Horn. Most museum customers didn't believe the story about the scalp, but they did believe the ball was real.

Why the museum had decided to sell the ball was suspect. At the board meeting they had looked at the books and decided that they would rather sell the ball then reduce the salary of the curator, Mrs. Pickwick. I had read a story in our local paper about the controversy. They described Mrs. Pickwick as a beautiful woman who met her husband when she was a dancer in Las Vegas. She was much younger than her husband when she married him. Her reputation for Helen of Troy beauty was widespread. She was a museum curator vixen.

Mrs. Pickwick's late husband had left a few of his not-so-hard earned dollars to the museum. He had been an attorney for a chemical company and died suddenly from a mysterious respiratory disease. Terry and I thought maybe it was caused by the fumes from the plant he represented. Some of the board members suspected that Mrs. Pickwick might someday leave the rest of the cash to the museum. If it was between Mrs. Pickwick's position and the ball exhibit, the baseball would have to go. Mrs. Pickwick had convinced the board that the museum needed more blue glass.

An unanimous vote, the board agreed to sell the ball. The three men on the board voted yes because they wanted the eye candy to stick around. The three women on the board wanted the money to buy glassware.

Terry called me the day he saw the article in the paper. The museum was going to put the ball on eBay and sell it. The casino in Nevada was going to buy it and put it on display in the lobby. The theme of the casino was called SEX and the exterior was crass, crude and tasteless. The showcase of the casino was a two story phallus that stood outside. Terry and I didn't want to know about the front door. The SEX Casino was no place for a baseball relic.

On one occasion Terry told me the story about how he had a personal encounter with the Babe. Terry was ten years old when he heard the news that the Babe was coming to his hometown. Ruth was on a barnstorming trip through the Midwest with a carnival baseball team. It was common for big league players to go on tour with a team and play local teams for amusement. Terry's dad was the groundskeeper for the park, so Terry got to be on the field and in the dugout when the Babe came to play. Ruth was having a bad-hip day, so he asked Terry if he could give him a hand with his spikes. So Terry got to help him lace up his spikes. He would describe it in great detail. His spade shovel hands. His Popeye forearms. Whenever Terry told the story I would just block out the fact that he was schizophrenic and that the whole thing might have been a story or a delusion or a folk tale. It didn't matter. It was real in my mind and that's all I needed.

I felt pretty special knowing a guy who met the greatest homerun hitter in baseball history. Terry was about 10 years old when he got to meet him. About the same age I was when I was in the library reading about the Bambino when I looked down and saw that not only was he a great hitter, but that he had the record for the most consecutive innings pitched without giving up a hit. I couldn't believe my eyes. Not only had he been the Sultan of Swat, but he was as good a pitcher as he was a hitter. At a young age Babe was my hero. And now Terry and I had to suffer the reality that a ball that he hit was going to be prostituted. We had decided that we were going to take action. We were going to steal the ball.

Terry, unlit pipe in hand, settled down in the ragged passenger seat.

"How ya doing?" I asked. "Ready to share a jail cell?"

"Whatever it takes, man," he replied. "At least I can plead insanity. What are you going to say?"

"I'll just tell them I work for a group home, and you're one of my clients," I said. "And yes—you can light up your pipe." I didn't care if he smoked in my car. I like the smell, and anything was better than my crusty old Chevy.

"Terrific cover. I get it. You are my group home provider," he said. "So how far is this Witro Museum, and how did they get the ball?"

"The ball was given to them."

"If we get caught," Terry mused, "we could just claim it's a plot for one of our books."

"Do you think that will work?" I queried.

"It's worth a try."

Our getaway car was not a getaway car. It was mainly an on-the-way-to-the-crime car. We were riding in a brown, rusted out '98 Chevy. My brother bought it from an Indian in South Dakota. It was a beauty. A rez car with that wonderful rez car sound, which city folks would call "no muffler." We were riding a war pony into battle. It was perfect for our job, and the South Dakota plates might throw off the authorities.

"How far is it?" Terry asked.

"About an hour and a half down highway 169."

Our brown beast was gliding down the highway. It rode close to the flat land. The highway was concrete, so every thirty yards where the cement had bulged the car would rise up and down like one of those ponies in an arcade ride. The bad shocks made the car dip, and the hood would rise up an inch or two. It was like sailing. The swells were hypnotic, and Terry and I both enjoyed it.

"Did I ever tell you about the time I was recruited by a Negro baseball team?" Terry said.

As I looked down the highway, with its bright white glow, I wondered if Terry had indeed become hypnotized.

"No, Terry, you didn't tell me you were recruited by a Negro baseball team," I said. "Unless I'm mistaken or you had some form of skin treatment, Terry, you are classically white."

He laughed, "No skin treatment. Really, they really talked to me about joining the team, and so I did."

"That kind of makes you a white Jackie Robinson, right?"

"Well, not exactly" he continued. "It wasn't one of the pro teams. It was a club team in Washington D.C. They saw me playing in a pickup game. I was shelling the pitchers pretty good, so they asked me, and I said yes."

With each story from Terry my mind would travel down the rabbit hole. I had to make an effort to process the story and determine whether it was real. In the end it was like a snare. I would just step in to the snare and wait for the rope to snap and grab my leg and send me up into the air. I took the bait every time because if I didn't he might not tell me another story.

I looked Terry in the eyes for some clue. I wondered if I should cross exam. After all what's wrong with a little detail?

"What position did they have you play?" I asked.

"They put me everywhere but usually centerfield. My nickname was "Snowball."

The Chevy was moving smoothly down the road. The beautiful Minnesota farm fields were a tunnel of corn. Most of the southern Minnesota natives knew that they really lived in Iowa. The state line was like Terry's reality.

"Snowball? Did they know you were from the north?"

"Yeah, one guy on the team, who was really black, was from St. Paul. I think he was Dave Winfield's grandpa. He looked like him."

The story was getting bigger, and I knew that the reference to the famous New York Yankee might be stretching it. I knew it was time to stop.

"You know, Terry, you should really write these stories down."

"Nah," he shrugged. "No one would believe them. I am crazy, you know. But you can use them if you want to."

We rode along in silence for quite awhile. It was one of those times when one doesn't know if one is moving or not. We were suspended in time. The road never changed, and the barns looked the same. Prairie highways are odd. There doesn't seem to be any traffic. All the other cars seem to have been beamed into space by aliens.

"Next week I'm going to see my psychiatrist. I see him once a month to see if he is alright. The last meeting I had with him he was doing very well."

"That's great, Terry," I said. "Do you have to pay him, or does he pay you?"

"Nah, he's at the VA. But that's a good idea. I will bring it up next time."

"Do you ever tell him about Babe Ruth or playing with a Negro team?" I chanced.

"He wouldn't believe me, so I don't talk about stuff like that. I did tell him that I was abducted by aliens, though."

"Really? And how did he deal with that?"

"He always just gives me more medication."

"Too bad," I said. "I wouldn't want that shit to ruin the story."

"No, the story never changes because it's true. I'll tell you about it sometime. Hey is this it?"

"Yeah, there it is. That green metal building. It looks like it should house John Deere tractors, not sacred baseballs."

"Let's get ready for the caper, partner," Terry said with a grin out of *Butch Cassidy and the Sundance Kid.*

When we walked into the place it looked promising. There didn't appear to be anyone minding the shop. Their hours were odd in that they were open on Tuesdays from 9 to 5. I don't know how many visitors they thought they would get. It was almost as if it was a front for some drug smuggling operation.

"Can I help you?"

There she stood. Mrs. Pickwick, the gorgeous curator we had heard about. She was breath taking in appearance. She was shapely and mature. She had a classy European look to her, and her voice was warm and inviting. She was pretty much what I had heard about. It was easy to see why the men on the board wanted her to stay.

"Well, hello," I said, trying to seem casual. "My name is Butch, and this is my friend Clyde. We have heard about your museum, and we wanted to check it out."

Terry picked up on my clever alias and chimed in.

"Yes, you must be Ms. Pickwick. We heard about you and your expertise in blue glass. We wanted to see some of it if you could spare us a few minutes."

"No problem at all. Let me show you our collection."

I jumped in right away, "Ms. Pickwick, excuse me, where is the men's room?"

"It's right down that hallway," she said with a nod and a smile.

"You guys go ahead. I will be along shortly," I replied, the plot moving me towards the ball which was displayed on the other side of the room.

It looked to me like I could just meander over to the display and put the ball in my pocket. It didn't seem to be the Great Train Robbery, but then we didn't need headlines. I first dipped into the restroom and then waited a few seconds and then poked my head out to see if Terry and Mrs. P. were still by the glassware. I crept out slowly and made my way towards the display case. The ball was sitting on the top shelf of the four foot high glass case. I would have to reach over and snatch the ball from behind. I knew my arm was long enough, and I knew I could slip the ball into my coat pocket.

Just as I was about to reach over Ms. Pickwick startled me, "Yes, indeed that is the Babe Ruth ball. I'd love to sell it to you, but it's already sold to a friend of mine from Las Vegas," she said, a little glimmer of pride in her voice.

"How much?" Terry asked. "If you don't mind me asking?"

"Oh, that's not public information yet because the paperwork hasn't gone through," Mrs. Pickwick said smoothly. "I can say that the selling price is more than enough for us to be the top blue-glass museum in the world."

"Wow. That's great, huh, Terry?"

"Yeah, great," Terry mumbled.

Terry could tell what my plan was, so I was hoping he would take the cue and get Mrs. Pickwick distracted. It didn't take him long and his dialog was perfect.

"Say Ms. Pickwick, the glassware and the ball are fascinating, but Butch and I are interested in purchasing the scalp of General Custer. Can we talk about that?"

"We sure can. Let's go into my office."

I ceased the moment, "Clyde, you go ahead. I'm going to catch a glimpse of that beautiful blue glass."

Mrs. Pickwick turned to Terry and said in the most seductive voice I have ever heard, "Come right this way." Jesus. She was Marilyn Monroe and Mae West rolled into one.

Minutes after Terry had gone in the office he came out and yelled to me in the back of the museum. I was slowly moving in on the ball when he yelled.

"Come on, Butch. We have to go."

The ride in the car north was quiet. We sat looking out the front window at the bobbing hood of the brown Chevy as we made our way back to our home town. The plan had not worked.

The car was somehow different now. It didn't seem quite so glamorous riding in a piece of junk on wheels. It wasn't a getaway car. We had failed. It was a shame car with two clowns in it. I waited for at least ten miles before speaking.

"So, Terry. Just what happened in that office that scared you?" I said. "I mean, did she have security cameras on or what?"

"No, nothing like that." Terry said. He seemed reluctant.

"Well, what was it?" I snapped. "I was seconds from grabbing the ball!"

"Sex!"

"What? What do you mean sex?" I was nearly screeching now.

"She said that she wanted to have sex with me."

I was shocked, "What? Are you kidding, Terry? Don't do this to me, Terry. Terry? Are you serious?"

Terry was breathing heavy, as if in a panic attack.

"No, I'm not kidding," he said. "She said she was attracted to me, and that she wanted me to get rid of you and come back, and we would screw on her desk."

"On her desk?" I was once again down the rabbit hole with Terry. "Terry, is this just a story? Are you off your meds? Because this is a bit farfetched."

"Believe me, this is not a story. I think she was a hooker in Vegas is what I think."

"Terry, a small town museum curator wants you to have sex with her in her office during business hours on her desk?"

"Hey! If she is a hooker, her business hours are 24/7. Seriously she wanted to do it right there on her desk. Creepy too because Armstrong Custer's scalp was right there next to the telephone."

Things had gone too far for me. I was no longer enjoying Terry's playful creative mind. The ball was still on its way to Vegas, and I was confused about reality. Like a converted Buddhist monk I came to the realization that the antidote for insanity was silence.

It seemed to be the road trip from hell. The ride back was twice as long. I needed to watch television or see a horror film. My brain needed to be engaged in a film fantasy, so I could establish what what was truly not real, so I could better understand what was.

Terry broke the silence, "Sorry, it just didn't seem right. I suppose I could have done it right there, and you could have taken the ball," he reasoned. "But I'm a married man. Would it be right for me to exploit the situation? I just couldn't let sex be a part of Babe Ruth."

I didn't respond. I just kept my eyes on the road and both hands on the wheel.

"Terry, do you mind if I put the radio on?"

He nodded as I reached and turned the knob.

A song came on, and I heard an opening line that I had never heard before from a group I didn't know. The line oft repeated was "Got a blank space where my brain should be."

I looked over at Terry, and he looked at me and said, "Did I ever tell you I was abducted by aliens?"

The Telltale Eleven

Pat Moriarity had been teaching English for over thirty years, and he was tired. Tired like one of those Thai elephants that haul logs all day. In his youth the lads in the neighborhood called him Paddy. Irish kids knew it was a nickname, but Protestant kids thought he was Patty like the girl's name. Or worse yet, Patty Cake. Fights ensued, so the nickname was dropped.

Pat was tired. Sometimes he would sigh and look up at the clock. He couldn't believe that he still had three more classes of American Literature. "Poe, Poe and more Poe forever more," was what he would tell Helen his wife when he got home. She felt sorry for him. She knew that he only had a few more months until retirement, and that the Twins season opener would be his elixir. Baseball had saved him in the past, and it would again.

Helen Moriarity was a gentle and fine woman. When her husband's students would meet her, they would nod approvingly. They could sense that she was the rock that made the marriage work.

Helen was a veterinarian. She and Pat met on the Moriarity family farm in Southern Minnesota. It had been love at first sight. Pat was working in the barn when his future wife came in to fix a sick cow. That's how it started.

She always had a way of making things work for the two of them. She had the innate ability to know what he needed.

"Pat, I bought tickets for the game," she said. "You and your brother should pick them up at will call."

Pat and his brother Danny had been Twins fans all their lives. They grew up in Bloomington, Minnesota, where the old stadium used to be and played ball with the Twins in their backyard, literally. They would play homerun derby at night by the light coming from the stadium across the street.

Helen spoke confidently, "Now listen. I'm going to my sister's house on Saturday while you and Danny are at the game. Do you think you can make it through Poe for one more week without burying me in the basement?"

"Very funny," he said. "But we finished *The Cask of Amontillado* last week. I'm on to *The Tell Tale Heart.*"

"Is that the one with the beating heart and the eye?"

"Yes, the kids love it."

"It stares at him, right?" She opened her eyes wide in mock terror.

"That's the one," he nodded. "I tell the kids that an obsession of that sort is the first step to insanity. Kind of like you and knitting," he chided.

"Hey, now you like those mittens, don't you?"

"Yes, I do," he said solemnly. "And the hats. And the sweaters . . ."

"Who's pitching for the Twins?"

"Twins pitching? What's *that*?" Pat responded sarcastically. "Do we even *have* a pitcher after Brocker's contract?"

Tom Brocker was the All-Star second baseman that the owner had offered the moon to at the expense of the rest of the team and the bull pen. There was no one out there because Brocker and his agent had taken all the money.

"Is he the one with the cute wife that you and your brother are always ogling?" she teased.

Pat shook his head. "She's okay. But it's Rodriguez' wife that's the looker. Man, she is a ten and a half. Danny goes to games just to see her."

"By the looks of the wives behind home plate, they're all gold diggers."

"Except now Brocker is the only one with the gold."

"I had no idea that you and Danny spent so much time looking at players' wives."

"Well, my brother is single," Pat pointed out. When Helen still looked disapproving, he added, "Oh, come on. It's good for a laugh. We are always looking for a fat ugly wife to show up, but it never happens. Must be a baseball thing, huh?"

"It's about the money, honey. That's why I passed up Derek Jeter and married you."

"Well, Jeter wasn't born yet, so maybe it could have been Mickey Mantle. But thanks for marrying me for my money."

"Have a good time," she said, giving him a quick kiss. "Say 'hi' to the wives for me."

Pat and Danny arrived early to great seats. The brothers liked to keep score, so they would arrive early to fill out their books. The scorebooks were a source of amusement for them because they would argue on every close play.

"Error on the shortstop!" Danny would bark.

"Clear base hit," Pat would argue.

Danny would put K's in the book for all strikeouts while Pat would put backwards K's for called third strikes. All of this was trivial to everyone but them. Senseless banter much like their running commentary on the looks of the players' wives behind them.

"Hey, Dan, here comes an ugly! Seriously," he said nodding subtlety.

"She's not a player's wife, you shmoe," Danny said, just as she turned into the section next to theirs.

"Guess you're right."

Pat looked up the aisle just as an entourage of beauties approached. Danny craned his neck to see the wives swanning around like runway models.

Pat saw Brocker's wife first. She wasn't beautiful but more perky-looking, like a college cheerleader. As they checked out the scenery, something bright caught their eyes.

"Look at that," Pat said. "That necklace."

The necklace was a museum piece. It was spectacular. Movie star stuff. It was big and round like a silver dollar. Embedded in the middle were diamonds that made the number 11. Brocker's number on the field. She was the wife of the Twins player who had signed a contact for more money than the team took in at the gate the previous year. And he wasn't even a Yankee.

Pat couldn't stop looking at the necklace.

"Oh my god! Even parts of the chain are diamonds," he said to his brother. "That thing must have cost a mint."

"Jesus, let it go and stop staring," Danny said. "She's going to think you are looking at her tits."

The announcer started with the line-ups, and the crowd got game ready. Pat tried not to look in the direction of the wives. He did, however, have a clear view of the necklace.

He was trying to fight off the obsession to stare at it. He compulsively took another quick glance, and his brother elbowed him, embarrassed.

"Quit looking, for god sake," Danny said. "You're a teacher. Have some dignity."

"I'm looking at that dang number 11," Pat said. "It's as big as a catcher's mask."

"Get over it and pay attention to your scorebook," Danny said.

"Fine," Pat replied, and turned to the back of the scorebook. On a blank page he drew the number 11. "This is how big the diamond thing is."

"Please," Danny said. "You're freaking me out here."

Pat had to admit that he was acting a little strange lately. The Twins' inability to sign a top notch pitcher? The end of the school year blues? Too much Edgar Allan Poe?

He thought of how he had discussed with his class the madman in the story *The Tell Tale Heart*. How the man was driven mad, not by events, but by his own mind.

"Listen to this excerpt," he had said to the room of bored students holding the heavy textbook in both hands. "I'm trying to get you hooked, so you finish the story for Monday. This is the lead character in the story, and I quote:

'You fancy me mad. Madman know nothing. But you should have seen me. You should have seen how wisely I proceeded—with what caution—with what foresight—with what dissimulation I went to. I was never kinder to the old man then during the whole week before I killed him.'

He set down the book on his desk.

"There you have it," he said. "Right there in the beginning of the story. That should keep you going. Poe is showing us a man who is suffering from a mental obsession." He lifted the book and read again:

Object there was none. Passion there was none. I loved the old man. He had never wronged me . . . For his gold I had no desire. I think that it was his eye.

"He goes on to describe the eye as an evil eye," Pat murmured, then resumed reading: "'*I saw it with perfect distinctness . . . all a dull blue, with a hideous veil over it that chilled the very marrow in my bones.*'"

He knew he was acting strange now. Right in the middle of his favorite thing in the world, and now he was thinking of work? Too much Poe probably was the problem. Though it could have been too much of anything after thirty years. Thousands of days standing in front of young people trying to convince them that they should read. Was it Poe or Brocker's wife that was causing him his own telltale nightmare on a Saturday afternoon at a baseball game?

"You okay?" Danny asked. "You don't look so hot. Do you want a Coke?"

"I'm fine," Pat said, rubbing his eyes. "I get this way whenever I teach Poe. You should see me when I'm on my Hemingway unit."

"What happens that week? Do you try to bullfight?"

"I'll be fine as soon as the Twins get out of this inning."

"Well, we're not even out of the first yet."

The White Sox had already scored four runs in the top of the first, and there were still no outs.

"Well, so much for our starting pitching," Danny groaned.

"I tell you, Danny. The general manager paid too much for a position player," Pat said, quickly tossing his head toward the cutie with the necklace. He had been trying not to look at her, so he could get over the necklace obsession, but it was not helping.

Over the next four innings, the Twins pitching hit an all-time franchise low. There was a virtual parade of relief pitchers. It became a horror show. By the seventh, half the crowd had left, and the score was an unbelievable 24 to 0.

"I can't believe this!" Pat said. "It's like a Poe short story. This is without a doubt the worst pitching staff in the history of baseball. I wouldn't give you a dime for the whole bunch."

"Wasn't that the point you were making in the first place?" Danny cracked. "The GM didn't give a dime for them. And please—easy on the Poe analogies. I'm trying to have fun here."

Pat looked at Brocker's wife again. He couldn't help but think of the evil eye of the old man as he looked at the diamond studded necklace.

"I'm telling you, Danny," Pat said in a low voice. "There are enough diamonds in that damn necklace for three or four quality pitchers, maybe even a lefty. By god, I bet you could get a Mario Rivera out of that damn thing." He was talking loud enough now for the people in the row in front of him to hear. They turned their heads and laughed in agreement.

He went on, realizing he was sounding more and more like a crank.

"Why the hell did he give all the money away for a stinkin' pendant?" he said. "It's all about conspicuous consumption. It's all about diamonds that people got killed for in Africa, while we could have had a real bull pen. I mean, why? It's just not fair. It's a Bud Selig kind of thing. Diamonds, diamonds, diamonds! Why? There is no justice!"

He was ranting and his brother was laughing but also shushing him to stop.

Just as he thought he was nearly over the edge there was a loud crack of the bat as a White Sox batter hit a three run homer.

"That's the ninth homerun this game." Pat lamented. "Danny, we are going to die here. This game will never end. We don't have anyone out there who can get this team out. We don't have a pitching staff! We have a jewelry store."

The small group of folks that could hear him only murmured now. The players' wives had little reaction on their part. Maybe they understood that it was just one game. A bad game, but they had seen bad games before.

Danny tried to calm his brother down.

"It's okay, man," he said. "Relax. There's always next year."

"You're right, Danny," Pat agreed. "I'm sorry. I was a victim of that evil eye. Hey, look. Brocker is up."

Brocker cracked a homer to leftfield that bounced into seats that had emptied out a few innings earlier. Danny and Pat both began to laugh as the infamous number 11 was trotting around the bases.

"There you go, Danny," Pat said. "Homerun. The score is now 27 to 1. *That's* what we paid our money for."

At that, they had had enough. They stood up and started moving out of the stands towards the exit. They were leaving the game before it was finished—something they had never done. Their scorebooks would be marked "incomplete" by the baseball gods. Their heads hung in shame as they trudged up the steps.

They both looked over at number 11's wife and noticed that she was smiling and applauding her husband's efforts. As she stood and applauded her necklace glistened with a blue light like the old man's eye in the story.

Patrick Moriarity came home that night with a heavy heart. He was like a beaten Viking warrior. He had lost the battle. He threw his scorebook aside and turned to go into his study. He stopped because he saw something on the kitchen table. It was a card and a small package. His lovely wife must have listened to the game on the radio. She was saintly, he thought. She had left him something to console him.

He opened the card first, it read: *To my favorite Irishman. Love, Helen.*

Pat opened the wee green package, and there looking up at him like a big green eyeball was a diamond shamrock ring.

The Sorcerer's Scorebook

I was kind of an oddity when I was a kid. All the kids called me Stats. I was the only person who liked to "keep the book." Keeping a baseball scorebook to me was kind of a religious experience. I loved the power of decision making. If I didn't like a kid on the team, I could give him an error on a really hot ground ball where other scorers would have scored a hit. The kids didn't know I was the book master. Nor did they care.

There is something mystical about penciling in doubles and triples and occasionally the joy of noting a 6-4-3 double play. The shortstop to second baseman to first baseman was such a cleansing in my book. It made my job that much easier. The strikeout throw out play was fun, too. The K would denote the strikeout and the 2-4 throw to second to get the base runner out was really exciting.

I guess it was the control that appealed to me, and I took to bringing my scorebook wherever I went. To school. To the corner store to buy gum. To the park. When I went up north to my grandparents' cabin one summer, along with my underwear and my baseball cards went the scorebook.

Up near my grandparents' cabin in Northern Minnesota, the Effie Mosquitoes were an amateur team who played summer ball in the Chippewa League. The league was a loosely affiliated group of teams that played out in the woods. It was pretty astounding to see a ball field out in the middle of the forest. We would drive for miles to a field that was in a green canyon of towering white and red pines. It would have been more natural to see bears on the field than pinstripes.

The Mosquitoes were a very competitive team, hoping to win the league championship, so they could go to St. Paul and play in the state tournament. The town of Effie only had four buildings on its main drag. I never really understood where all the players came from. I used to imagine that they were all aliens. That a spaceship landed outside of town, and when the hatch opened, a row of baseball players marched out of it and headed for the nearest diamond.

My scorebook was not the official book, but it looked official. I got it from an exclusive baseball store near Wrigley Field. It was larger than most books, and so it got the attention of other scorers. The book was a jewel. It had large boxes that let me make huge K's when someone struck out.

One day the Mosquitoes were playing the Walker Wolves in a tight match. A pop up drifted behind third, and the third baseman, the shortstop and the leftfielder were in pursuit. As the player pulled in the ball, the crowd clapped, and I moved my pencil into the appropriate box and noted F-6 for fly ball caught by the shortstop.

My grandpa, who continually gave me unsolicited advice, corrected me.

"That wasn't the shortstop. It was the third baseman."

I acknowledged the mistake and began to erase the mark. But before I had completed my correction, the announcer broke in with, "The catch was made by Baker, the shortstop." I stopped erasing and looked at my grandpa, who just laughed.

"You were right again, sonny boy."

I smiled and moved on to the next hitter.

The next batter was a big Swede named Gustafson who had struck out previously. He was called out on strikes. My grandpa and I got in a big discussion as to whether I should put a backwards K for a strikeout looking. I told him it didn't matter, but he insisted it did. I relinquished and started making backwards K's for called third strikes.

As expected, Gustafson struck out looking again, so I put the backwards K in place and got ready for the next batter, a big Indian named Goldtooth.

After all the debate about K's and backwards K's, I was a bit flustered. I prided myself in pristine pages in my book. A perfect game to me was no mistakes in the scorebook. No eraser marks, no missed K's, no missed errors instead of hits. The book had to be right. I don't really know why. I suppose I wanted the approval of the baseball gods. I wanted to be as good with my book as Willie Mays had been in centerfield. Baseball fans have a responsibility.

I believed that—still do. People bring that responsibility with them to the ballpark. If everyone in the ballpark has done the right thing, the team wins. If someone messed up on the way to the game, it affects the outcome. If Bill or Bob or Bud made a wrong turn and missed the first batter, that could annoy the baseball gods enough to cause the rightfielder to let the ball run through his legs to the fence.

To my dismay I looked down in my book and saw that I had mistakenly put the K for Gustafson below in Goldtooth's spot in the book.

"Look what you made me do, Grandpa," I sighed. "I put it in the wrong box."

Grandpa looked up.

"Hey, wait a minute," he said. "Maybe it will be all right. Goldtooth can't lay off that outside pitch. He'll probably strike out, anyway."

I was trying to remain calm and mature as an official scorer should, but I was losing my composure.

"Yeah, but if he swings, it will still be wrong because I put a backwards K down," I said.

I heard the umpire, who was also an Indian, snap, "Strike three! You're out!" Goldtooth was out, and my book was correct. Perfect.

My grandpa and I laughed and enjoyed our perfection. The Mosquitoes were ahead 7 to 0. The pitcher, Rory Reiter, was on a roll with six straight strikeouts. It was getting late in the game, and we were hoping that my Grandpa's friend Yank would get in the game as a pinch hitter. Yank was his first and last name, and everyone loved him. He was a house painter in town, and this was his last year with the team. He had been a Cubs minor league player in his youth, which was reason enough to like the guy.

Yank was fading fast. He was a leather-faced Sherpa in a baseball uniform. He looked 100. I thought he probably played with Babe Ruth. Grandpa assured me that he wasn't that old, and that he was still a deep threat. I was kind of surprised that a guy so old could still play. It made me appreciate just how good the Cubs were even if they spent most of their time in the cellar of the National League. Yank couldn't break into the big leagues, but he played for twenty years in the minors. Here he was with a rinky-dink town team. I hoped he'd still be able to produce.

Yank came in as a pinch hitter, and the crowd responded with applause and encouragement. He was the town favorite, and to many in this older crowd,

Yank represented the older generation. Yank was Patton, Eisenhower, Lindbergh, Jack Dempsey and the rest of the giants of the glory days. My grandpa was excited and gave me a loving pat on the shoulder as if to say, "Watch this."

Yank took a pathetic swing at a curveball and fell down. I felt bad for him. He looked foolish. His swing was something you might have seen from some kid who was from a land far away from baseball. I had a terrible feeling in my stomach.

"Strike two!" was the call from the Indian umpire.

My grandpa had a look on his face like he was going to die. I was afraid that he was having a heart attack. Trying to distract him, I nudged him and took my pencil and found Yanks' box in the book. I motioned to him to look next to Yanks' name where I penciled in a homerun. I drew a line from home to first to second to third and home again. A perfect diamond. HR. A homerun.

My grandpa smiled and put his arm around my shoulder. He knew I was trying to help in any way I could.

"Ball one," the ump called.

"Well, sonny boy," my Grandpa said. "He's still in it."

Yank took the next two pitches, so the crowd was back in it. He was at a full count. This was it. The battle for the wood. The cheeky youth and the dignified old Cub.

The ball left the pitcher's hand, and it was moving below speed gun detection. It was moving so slow that the word velocity couldn't be used. He had definitely taken something off the pitch. It was so sluggish, my grandpa leaned over and said, "Bolo ball! It's a trick pitch. He's trying to strike him out with a trick pitch!"

My grandpa was infuriated. Yank was getting no respect from this upstart.

Yank moved his feet back and readied himself for the bolo ball. His spine could be heard unwinding as he sprung. His bat was moving so fast that many of us thought he had dropped it. The sound of the ball hitting the bat sounded like deep-seated angst.

Grandpa was on his feet. I dropped my scorebook. The fans were gasping air, sucking in their breath for a monster exhalation of tension. The ball was headed for the Van Amber Timber sign in centerfield, 405 feet. The fielder stood still, and in an act of respect he bowed to Yank while reaching down to take a strand of grass to chew on. The ball was over the fence in seconds. We would later learn that it came to rest on the train tracks, 455 feet away. The crowd was hysterical. Yank was moving around the baselike he had done this as many times as the Babe himself. My grandpa sat back down, wiping his forehead. Smiling enough that his face might crack, his generation vindicated.

I moved from the bleachers to crawl underneath for my scorebook. It was hostile territory fighting my way through discarded cups and old programs and peanut shells. My book was lying open with a splinter of light on Yanks page. There it was the prophetic HR for the monster shot that we all enjoyed.

My grandpa and I drove back to his cabin in his ancient pickup he called "Old Blue." We were laughing about my scorebook and how it was too bad the Cubs didn't have one.

"If they had a book like mine maybe they could win the World Series." I said.

"Oh, look it there, sonny boy!" He pointed. "A black bear."

Up the road to the left, sure enough, there was the burly bear, tall as a totem pole. As if the day hadn't been exciting enough. I was eager to get back to the cabin to tell my mom that I had seen a big black bear. I could write about it in the cabin journal.

I could write, *Today I saw a burly black bear.*

Or maybe I'd write, *Today grandpa and I were able to flush out a 600 pound man killer.*

Or, *Yank had hit a homerun to the moon and back.*

When it was time to go back to Chicago, I took a look at my scorebook and threw it in my suitcase. I felt sad about leaving my grandparents. I might not see them until Christmas, and with my grandpa getting older I was always afraid he was going to die. Could Grandpa hold on until we got to see a pack of wolves? Or maybe just a couple of wolves? That would be special.

When I got back to the heat in Chicago, I kept the story of my book a secret. The whole thing scared me, but my grandpa told me not to worry about it.

"It was just a call," he said. I called a homerun and Yank got one. "That's all there is to it, sonny boy."

Even so, when my mom went to work at night I would get my scorebook out and watch the Cubs on TV. I started experimenting with my book. I started innocently enough with writing in a bunt single for Forbes or maybe a stolen base for Flaherty. I would wait for a few pitches and then I'd write SB for stolen base, and Flaherty would be off and running, "safe."

At first I figured it a coincidence. I knew these players so well, maybe I was just anticipating their next moves. But I kept trying it, and it seemed like my scorebook was predicting the outcomes. It was almost addictive, marking down my hopes and then seeing them translate onto our TV screen. I felt more like I was one of the baseball gods. I even put down stuff for the St Louis Cardinals. If they were behind by three or more, I'd write in HR for Rodriguez just for fun. I never let them win though.

The problem was that I wasn't sure if it was the book or me. Sometimes I wouldn't write a hit in the book. I would just concentrate on a hit for Gibson and not write it down. I mean, I would really concentrate like when I was in church praying. But it didn't matter how hard I concentrated. Gibson ground out to the second baseman like he always did.

Whether or not the book would work on someone else was not on the table. I didn't care. No one else was going to find out about my book.

My life was becoming complicated with the knowledge that this book could bring the Cubs the World Series. The problem was whether I had enough pages to bring them a pennant. They would have to win at least 90 games and that was not something they could do easily.

I decided to look at the schedule and make up my win list. I thought if I could win 34 key games that might bring them over the top. I would ration the wins and keep four pages for the World Series. Secrecy was a key component of the plan. I also didn't know if I had to be at the games or even watch them. I was also going to experiment with individual plays versus the whole game.

I still remember the second game after the All Star game. I took the Cubs and Braves, and I penciled in the whole game. I gave Shultz, the pitcher for the Cubs, a one-hitter (but I kept him with a no hitter—couldn't resist!—into the eighth). I gave the Cubs a one-run victory on a wild pitch in the ninth inning. I don't know why, but I felt like I had to be subtle with the outcome. Writing in no-hitters or grand slams would have just been greedy.

I watched the game on TV with my book sitting on the foot stool in front of me. I would look at my book once and awhile to see if the game was following the script in my scorebook. Indeed, it was. I was onto something.

Many people would look at the magic as evil, but if you're a Cubs' fan there is no such thing as evil if it means the Cubs win. Even though I was young I had already been subjected to all of the stories about how Satan and all of the fallen angels were spending too much time messing up the Cubs. I used to look at the stained glass images in church of the devil and his black army and think that the Cubs never had a chance with all these evildoers working for the Cardinals. And the Braves. And the Philly's . . . Working for every baseball team against the Cubs.

It was September, and I was managing along with the bullpen to put a few games in the win column for the Cubbies. I have to give them credit—they were doing most of it themselves, but whenever there was a chance of a two-game swing with the league-leading Cardinals, I would write out the game. I tried to help out the Cardinals players as well. If someone was struggling at the plate I'd have them go 4 for 4 but still have the Cardinals lose. I tried to give the pitching losses to new guys who had just been brought up. I thought management would be more patient with them. None of it really mattered. What mattered was that the Cubs would win.

Late September came and a huge series with the league-leading Cardinals was going to make the difference in winning the pennant. I was plotting out my strategy for the Saturday game. Much to my disappointment the game wasn't going to be televised. I was really disheartened, but I remained professional and realized that it didn't matter. I could listen to it on the radio. I was plotting out how the game would play out when the kitchen phone rang.

It was my grandmother, and she had some big news. She handed the phone to my grandpa.

"Well, sonny boy, how would you like to go to the Cubs' game with your grandpa?"

I think it was ten minutes later when my mom stroked the back of my neck that I finally came back into the room. My Grandpa's invite had sent me reeling a wee bit. For some reason my mind flashed on he and I hiking in the woods of Minnesota last winter.

"There they are, sonny boy," he said, breath coming like frost in the cold.

I had looked up and staring at us in the falling snow were two wolves.

My mother said, "I don't think I have ever seen you speechless."

I had to take the phone and say good bye.

"Were you thinking about the game?" my Mom asked.

"No, I was thinking about timber wolves," I said, realizing it sounded crazy.

My mother smiled and said, "Maybe at Christmas. Now get to bed. Grandpa and Grandma are staying tonight out by the airport. Grandpa is going to pick you up at noon. Try to sleep."

The pressure was numbing. I had a big game, and I had to make sure I didn't blow it. I decided to take a situational approach to the game. If the Cubs were up by 10 runs, I didn't have to squander the page. I could just leave some of the book blank and then use the last few innings later. I'd have to hope that no one in the press would notice that the first four innings were the same as a week's earlier. It was all very complex, but it didn't matter because it was my secret and mine alone. Grandpa might be a problem, but I could keep the book out of his sight.

It was a beautiful day at Wrigley. We were in leftfield, and I couldn't have been happier. My grandpa got the tickets from a ticket broker friend of his, an Irish gangster named Paddy Murphy. He use to rob banks, but Grandpa said he got tired of that, so now he was a scalper. I never knew if the stuff my Grandpa told me was real or imagined. He had a thing for stories. I didn't care. I loved the stories, and I would get really mad when people would challenge him. It didn't matter. I'd keep his eyes off the book.

The game was too close to mess around. I was trying to keep it close, so Grandpa would enjoy the game and then be able to tell the story of it, so everyone knew it was true.

The Cubs were playing a flawless game. I was proud of them, and if it hadn't been so late in the season I might have backed off and let them take it alone, but it was too critical. We had to win.

It was the bottom the ninth, and the score was tied. They had to do something. Something not . . . Cublike, something that wouldn't result in what they always did—lose. Grandpa could hardly contain himself.

"Sonny boy, I think I'm going to wet my pants," he said. "You think you could make a call like you did with Yank back in Effie?"

"Grandpa, I don't think I have to," I said. "We have Juan Juan up."

The crowd was fidgety, sitting on a moment that could be revolutionary. Could this be the year? The atmosphere was odd, as if we were all in some kind of decompression chamber.

Juan Juan glided into the batter's circle. He was a Dominican of heroic stature. On the island he was a god.

The Dominicans were so in love that they gave him two first names as if he were two giants in one frame. He was taking his practice swings, and the crowd noise was beginning to mount. My hands were shaking so much I couldn't afford to wait. I opened the book and found my place. Two outs in the ninth. Juan Juan at bat. I made sure I had the right box, paused and with a deliberate action I put HR in the box. I then made the diamond lines and filled in the box that would bring the Cubs victory. My grandpa leaned in to see if I had made a prediction, but I closed the book at the last second. He smiled. He knew I had marked the end of the game in the Cubs favor. I made it a first pitch homerun because I couldn't stand another thriller.

The pitcher, who wasn't privy to my book, was going to get ahead in the count by piping a fast ball. Juan Juan was ready and able. The smoke came pouring out of the pitcher's hand, and Juan Juan swung a fraction early making sure the fat of the bat, the meat of the maple, the nuclear center, would connect with the ball, and so it did.

The sound put the thirty thousand people on the launching pad.

5. . . 4. . . 3. . . 2. . . 1. . .

And they were up. The ball, practically oblong at this point from the force, was headed straight up and out like the entire space agency. It was a no-doubt shot. We watched with our mouths gaping open like the lens of a camera at Camp Canaveral. I could see the ball and behind it the stars and stripes of the greatest country in the world, but something was wrong . . . dreadfully wrong.

The flag was suddenly alive and up with the crowd and blowing in. Blowing in. Not blowing out.

"Grandpa, is it going to make it?" I said.

The centerfielder from the Cardinals was in some sort of dream state because he obviously didn't know about my magic book. He had a bead on the ball. He could actually see it, and something inside his tiny brain made him think he could catch it. He was running for the finish line ahead of the Olympic field, and at the same time he was leaving the playing field. He was Jordanesque in his leap for the ball.

Thwack!

I swear I could hear the ball hit his glove, and then a hideous sound of a body hitting a brick wall.

"He caught the ball," I whispered. Then I was shouting. "Grandpa, he caught the ball!"

I opened my book "Look! I have Juan getting a homerun. This is impossible."

"Look, son. Juan is running the bases."

Juan Juan was frantically running the bases as if he were trying to complete an inside-the-park homerun. I had no idea what was happening.

"You did it, sonny boy!" my Grandpa shouted. "The umpire just signaled homerun! Cubs win, sonny boy! Cubs win!"

The crowd was rollercoasting along with the massive stroke of a bat, a run and a catch for the Hall of Fame, and then a signal from the umpire that the Cubs had indeed won regardless of the catch. The Cubs dugout erupted with joy. The players were mobbing Juan Juan who was safely out of the base paths.

In centerfield we could see a crowd of players and first aid personnel. Several players and coaches were verbally assaulting the umpires who had formed a protective huddle around their crew chief. The rest of the people in the stands didn't need explanations. The Cubs were in first place and would surely be on to the playoffs.

"Grandpa, what happened?" Grandpa had been talking to a guy next to him that had been listening on the radio. "Well, sonny boy, the guy on the radio said that although the ball was caught, the man who catches it has to release it or throw it back in. I guess the guy who caught it is out cold and on his way to the hospital."

I was quiet on the way home. I guess it's one thing winning a ball game. It's another thing having a guy unconscious in a hospital. Grandpa was kind of confused about my reaction.

He said, "I admire your concern, but it's not like you were responsible. Things like that happen. It's Wrigley Field. There's a brick wall behind the Ivy. Everyone knows that." I just sat silently and watched the brownstone buildings of Chicago pass by. People were joyous, waving banners, honking horns, celebrating. I, on the other hand, was bearing the full responsibility of causing a man to be close to death.

When we got back to the house my mother was all excited and giving me kisses and hugs. I said, "Yeah, it's great the Cubs won but there's a man in the hospital." My mom and my grandparents were surprised by my reaction and were already plotting out a new life for me where instead of being the manager of the Cubs I would instead win the Nobel Peace Prize. They were impressed by my compassion.

Little did they know that my secret was a booby prize. I had drawn the guilt card out of the stack. I had only one choice. I had to burn my book. Exorcise the demons that had taken a good thing and made it evil. A Cubs win or a human life. It was a critical time in my development.

The open air fire pit was in the backyard. We rarely used it because of some new law, but it didn't matter to me. I grabbed some tissue paper and some charcoal lighter and proceeded to the backyard. A scorebook cremation ceremony was needed to purge the guilt from my being. And the baseball deity would say, "Yes, my son, it is finished."

Just as I was about to light the pyre, my mother yelled out the window.

"Honey, the radio says that Eckko is day-to-day. He's going to be okay."

"What?" I yelled. "Who's okay?"

"Eckko, the Japanese player of the Cardinals? He's fine. You can relax now. Come back in the house and give your grandparents a hug."

Eckko is day to day were the sweetest words I had ever heard. Not only was he not dead, but he would be playing soon. I felt like a new person. I had been vindicated. I was free at last. Oh, those words. *Day to day.* It was almost as good as *pitchers and catchers report.*

But I still had my crisis: the book.

I tried to get the smell of the fluid off the book, but I was still unclear if I wanted to keep it and go through the agony of the last few hours. I said good bye to my grandparents, and we talked about coming out at Christmas, so I could have a go at finding those wolves again. As their car sped off I knew I had a decision to make. I couldn't share it with my mother because I had been given a special gift, and it was my decision alone to make.

I sat on the front porch for a long time and contemplated the pros and cons of destiny. Should the Cubs win? Why was I given this burden? I collected my thoughts and moved up the steps, through the front door and up the steps to my room.

I took some brown wrapping paper from my drawer, and I carefully wrapped the relic. I took a marker, and I wrote on the outside of the paper: *Magic Scorebook: Use for Cubs in the World Series ONLY.* I hiked up the attic stairs to my baseball collection, opened up the trunk and put the book on the bottom.

The following Christmas my Grandpa and I were walking in the Chippewa National Forest, and we saw two beautiful timber wolves. They stopped, turned their heads to look at us, and then turned and walked away. They were a gift.

My Grandpa died the following week of a heart attack. On his tombstone it said, *Here Lies The Storyteller.*

We loved the stories and the storyteller. My relatives tell me that I'm like my Grandpa and now they call me The Storyteller. This has been my story, *The Tale of the Sorcerer's Scorebook*. Someday, when the Cubs win the World Series, you will know how they did it.

Patrick Ryan is a freelance writer and teacher from Mankato, Minnesota. He has authored several nonfiction books for children as well as three plays and several screen plays. He is currently working on an adult novel entitled *I Didn't Put Honey in the Soap Disperser* and a screenplay entitled *Our Lady of the Pub*. This is his first book of short stories.

Special Thanks to Jim Van Amber, Carrie Mesrobian, Terry Davis, John Bonnes, Kathy Steiner, John Kind, Jo Ann Haney, Tom Peterson, Tim Horan, Ron Peck, Gary Parker, Steve Potts, Isaac Dog Eagle, Dennis Blue, Brian Strapp, Matt Wertz, Zillah Glory, Dan Ostlund, Mitch Petrie, JJ, Becky Poole, Blake Hoena, Bryana Cook, Patrick Evan, Katie and James Martens, Daniel Paul Ryan, and the Marysbourg Group.

CPSIA information can be obtained
at www.ICGtesting.com
Printed in the USA
FFOW05n1026170115

9 780981 827940